Father Jeremy

Jim Connelly

Other Books by Jim Connelly

Tom and Anna on the Trail: the Case of the Missing Schoolgirl (2014)

Tom and Anna in Danger: the Case of the Disappearing Dogs (2014)

Tom and Anna take a Chance: the Case of the Bungling Bird Bandits (2015)

My Folk: Four Hundred Years of Hazards, Tooths, and Connellys (2015)

Mountain Boy (2016)

Talk of the Town: Warragul/Drouin (2017)

Talk of the Town (2): Warragul/Drouin (2018)

Pickled Pieces and Rollicking Rhymes (2019)

Wild Beauty (2019)

Round and About in Gippsland (2020)

Father Jeremy

Copyright

A CIP catalogue record for this book is available from the National Library of Australia

First published in Australia 2020 by
James Timothy Connelly
12 Craig Street,
Warragul, Victoria, 3820
AUSTRALIA
ajcon@dcsi.net.au

For the Clergy of the Diocese of Gippsland, past and present

Cover design by Craig Braithwaite, *aussiepics*

Contents

Foreword

Let me introduce my friend, Father Jeremy. I needn't say much about him, actually. His character comes through on every page of this book. Like many of us, he relies a great deal on his partner. Indeed, this book is almost as much about Josie as it is about Jeremy. Bear with our friend in his travails and in his modest successes. Like all of us, he has his strong and his weak points, but unlike some of us, he always has good intentions.

Maybe you'll want to know the end of the story. Jeremy saw out his three extended years of ministry in the parish as strongly and warmly as ever. At his farewell, he was given a set of golf clubs and a pair of reclining armchairs. The clubs are in full use; the chairs await their time. Jeremy and Josie moved not far away. They see quite a bit of their old friends, but are careful not to interfere with the work of their successor. The last I saw of them, Jeremy and Josie were coping well with the coronavirus lockdown, and were looking forward to resuming their volunteer work with the Hospital Auxiliary.

Jim Connelly, October, 2020.

Antoinette

Father Jeremy was worried. Antoinette hadn't arrived for church. It was the Thursday morning service, and the usual dozen people were assembled, sitting quietly in their pews waiting for him to begin the service. But not Antoinette.

The cause of his anxiety was that last Sunday, as she was leaving after the morning service, she had said something he hadn't understood. Antoinette had been talking to him about the morning's reading from one of Paul's letters. 'There's too much said about substitutionary atonement,' were her words as she walked away.

Antoinette was clever. She read serious books, and particularly books of theology. She knew what substitutionary atonement was, obviously, but Father Jeremy was not too sure. His theological college days were in the distant past. He remembered the phrase, but just what it meant was something that had passed from his mind over his long years of ministry.

'Substitutionary atonement'? What had he done wrong to have her say that to him? To Father Jeremy, ministry was a simple calling: read the Bible and tell his people of its message; help them in their daily lives; be there when they needed support and encouragement; and pray with them and for them. Where did this 'substitutionary atonement' fit into that?

Antoinette hadn't been in the parish very long. Jeremy was unsure about her. Was she going to unsettle the even tenor of his ways? Was she going to influence others so that people would think he should be doing things differently? People had always spoken about 'Good old Father Jeremy'. Would they want someone else, someone who was theologically astute, someone who could quote the Bible in Hebrew or Greek, someone who preached half-hour sermons?

These things had been gnawing away at Father Jeremy since Sunday. Antoinette's comment, tossed over her shoulder as she walked away, had unnerved him. And now she hadn't turned up for church. Jeremy could feel the certainties of his life crumbling away.

He worried about Antoinette herself, too. She was a single woman, who appeared to enjoy the company of others in the church. She needed to stay with them for her own sake, it seemed to him.

He picked up his Prayer Book and moved towards the Narthex to begin the service. As he did so a shadow from the front door caught his eye. It was Antoinette. Something moved within his chest. He paused, giving her time to take her place. But instead of going straight into church, she came towards him.

'Sorry I'm late,' she said. 'The phone rang at the wrong time. I've run all the way. Couldn't miss church, you know.' And she gave him the sweetest smile he had ever known.

Father Jeremy's heart leapt within him. He paused for a moment. Antoinette's smile had said more than words. What matter substitutionary atonement now? Father Jeremy felt his spirit lift heavenward. He bowed his head. 'Thank you, Lord,' he muttered, and strode into the church with unusual certainty.

'The Lord be with you,' he began. 'And also with you,' the people replied. He noticed Antoinette's voice above the rest.

Father Jeremy's Christmas Pageant

It was the first Sunday of December, and Sunday School was in full rehearsal for the Pageant on Christmas Eve. The highlight, as always, would be the Crib scene.

The parts were chosen – Mary and Joseph, the angels, the shepherds, the sheep, the donkey, the cows. The innkeeper role was strongly contested, but, in a master-stroke of decision-making, Ian was chosen because his name almost spelt 'Inn'. The children voted unanimously to have a kangaroo in order to give an Australian touch to the event. The loser in the Innkeeper event, Brian, was handed this role in another clever tactical move. All seemed set, except that one matter remained undecided, and that was the most important of all …

'You'll have to make the decision, you know, dear,' Josie began.

Father Jeremy's head appeared above the morning paper. 'Decision?' he murmured indecisively. 'Can't you do it?' he replied.

'Not this time,' said Josie. 'It's the Baby. Who's going to be the Baby Jesus?'

Jeremy sighed a deep sigh.

It was a long-standing tradition of the parish that the part of Baby Jesus would be played by a live baby.

This year there was deep rivalry between two mothers for the role to fall to one of their beloved infants. Josie went on, 'You must decide – and soon, before the feeling festers and open war breaks out.'

Father Jeremy put his paper down. There was silence for some time, as Jeremy thought through the possibilities. Eventually he spoke. 'The last baby in the parish to be baptised will be Baby Jesus,' he pronounced with an air of finality. 'Then there can be no argument. That is the Law of the Medes and Persians. I'll ring Molly straight away.' Molly was the hard-working Sunday School superintendent.

Jeremy turned to go to his study, but was held by a discreet cough from Josie. Jeremy knew that kind of cough.

'Twin girls,' said Josie. 'Don't you remember? Those little twin girls. They were the last ones baptised. You can't have two baby Jesuses.' Jeremy was stopped in his tracks. 'What do the Medes and Persians say about that?' Josie added, with unusual acidity.

Back in his study, Jeremy wished he could ask King Solomon for help. Hadn't he had to decide on a dispute about a baby? Then he remembered Solomon's suggestion - the baby be cut in two - and quickly abandoned that line of thought.

But Jeremy's fertile mind went to work. A conference between the Superintendent, the mother, and himself was hastily arranged. Jeremy's diplomacy was superb. The meeting ended with smiles all round.

And so when the curtain went up on Christmas Eve, it turned out that not only Mary, but also the kangaroo had that night given birth. One of the twin girls was safely deposited on Mary's lap, while the other was placed in Brian's brawny arms, hidden as they were beneath his kangaroo suit.

Father Jeremy had to agree – and Josie too. It was the best Christmas pageant ever.

The Old Folks at Home

There was an Aged-Care residential home in the parish, attached to the hospital. Every second Wednesday morning, Father Jeremy arrived to conduct the eleven o'clock service. Sister Irene would bring the old people in their wheelchairs.

He had a mixed congregation of a dozen or so, of various and unknown denominational background.

Today, Sandra from the church had come to play for them, so there was some attempt at singing. Rita called out her choice of songs, as always. Her choice was very limited – either *There is a green hill far away* or *I Walked in the Garden Alone* – and as there was no competing bid they sang one to begin with and the other at the end.

Jeremy rather liked the second one actually. His imagination always dwelt on the third line, "And the voice I hear falling on my ear". He would place a comma after 'I hear' which gave a secret and rather comic twist to the meaning.

James was the keenest participant. Today he had brought along a reading. It was from Bishop Green's 'Daily

Meditations', published 1888. There was one full page for each day of the year, in small print.

As he finished, a furrow crossed James's brow. 'Oh,' he said. 'I read yesterday's by mistake. Here's the right one,' and started off again.

Sister Irene came to the rescue. Sister Irene was a darling. 'You read it to me after the service, James,' she called out, 'when the others have gone.'

Saved the day! Jeremy gave her a silent blessing.

The Bible reading Jeremy had chosen was the miraculous draft of fishes.

No matter what the reading, Jeremy's 'sermon' always came round to the same message – that we should love one another as God loves us, and forgive one another as Jesus taught us to.

This morning's address was extended, however, by Violet, who launched on a considerable excursus about a boat, her father, a lemon tree, and walking two miles to school through the frost.

The others looked most unforgivingly at her (lunch followed the service), and eventually they moved on to the Communion.

As he dipped the host into the wine and placed it on each proffered tongue, Jeremy's heart went out to each of them. He felt a pang of shame for his earlier impatience, and gave each a silent blessing.

 As an act of contrition, he stayed back to listen to James's reading with Sister Irene.

Afterwards, he had a quiet word with Irene. 'They're all beautiful,' said Jeremy, 'and content with who they are. They're past worrying about putting on a false front.'

'There's someone looking after each one of them,' Irene said, cryptically.

As he drove home, Jeremy said a prayer of thanksgiving for being able to minister to these people.

Josie noticed his air of introspection. 'A nice service?' she enquired. Jeremy nodded.

'All there?' Josie went on.

'All there,' Jeremy echoed. 'A dozen of the old folk and a large contingent of angels.'

Street Talk

Jeremy knew quite a few of his colleagues who spent much of their time in the street. 'That's my parish,' David, had said to him at the last Deanery meeting. 'If the people don't come to the church, I'll take the church to the people,' he'd added.

Jeremy always felt a shadow of doubt when he heard others talk like that. 'It's not my style,' he said to Josie, though Josie had gone on beating the eggs and said nothing in reply. 'I'm not an extrovert,' Jeremy went on, 'like that David'.

It happened that Jeremy had to go to the Post Office one Saturday morning not long after this exchange had taken place. A parcel from Scripture Union was waiting for collection. It was a sunny morning and Jeremy was quite pleased to stroll down to pick up his package.

He was away for a long time. When he arrived home, Josie noticed a warm flush on his face. 'Interesting people, those McAlisters,' he said, immediately. 'Told me all about their time in Indonesia … and their son and daughter-in-law are coming back to live here. Remember them?'

Josie said nothing, but Jeremy went on. 'It's interesting who you bump into. There was a chap outside the hardware store. We got talking. He did some work on the church roof before we came. Knew all about the church.'

'Uh-uh, muttered Josie. 'Coffee?' she asked, 'or will you wait for lunch?'

'Sorry,' Jeremy replied. 'I actually had some down the street. In that place in the Arcade. Flat white. Beth and Norman were there and asked me to join them. Norman goes on long-service leave in July. They're thinking of getting a caravan and going north.'

Josie was smirking. 'Anything else?' she asked.

'It's quite a social place, that Arcade,' Jeremy continued. 'You'd never think how many people go through there. They're a nice lot, aren't they!'

'I don't know,' Josie replied. 'I don't spend much time sipping flat whites in the Arcade.'

Jeremy threw her a look. 'Well, they looked nice people … and a lot of them gave me a smile as they went past.'

'That will be because of your collar,' Josie commented. Jeremy always liked to wear his clerical collar in public. 'It flies a little flag,' he used to say.

'So you had quite a convivial morning,' Josie went on. 'Anything else?'

'Well, it's really amazing, but I came across Bert Hutchings just here on our corner. He's going in to get a pacemaker on Tuesday. Just as well he told me. Nobody else would have, now he's on his own.'

Josie put her hands on her hips. 'Now, Mister Father Jeremy,' she said, 'What did that David say about the street being his parish? Not your style, I think you said. You're not an extrovert. No, not you!'

Jeremy shook his head.

"And the parcel?' Josie added.

A look of horror spread across Jeremy's face. 'The parcel! I forgot all about it!

'Never mind,' he laughed. 'It can wait till Monday.'

The Wrong Door

Jeremy was a little anxious.

He'd heard that some new people had come to live in Gordon Street and they had some connection with the church. Number 29, he'd been told. Still, this didn't seem right. The front yard was full of clutter, and there was the unmistakable sound of a hen laying an egg somewhere behind the house.

There being no answer to his ring at the front door, he edged round the side of the house, feeling like an intruder.

He found a woman – fortyish – cleaning something in a chook run. She had her back to him. 'Hallo,' he called in his practised unthreatening way. She jumped, then laughed.

Through the wire fence, the conversation quickly demonstrated that the new people lived next door at Number 31, but the woman, observing his clerical collar, seemed more than prepared for a chat.

'I'm not a churchgoer, but I'm a believer,' she said. (How many times had Jeremy heard that!) 'I know there's someone up there' (waving her hand vaguely skywards). 'I've been there.'

This *did* interest Jeremy. 'Been there?' he asked.

The woman – 'Toni', she quickly volunteered – went on to explain in a down-to-earth way, how she had experienced a near-death experience some years earlier when giving birth to her first child.

'Near-death?' Jeremy encouraged her in his best CPE manner.

Briefly, Toni explained. There had been a glow of white light surrounding her. She felt infinitely assured, infinitely peaceful. She didn't see God as a figure, a person, but as a presence, more as great source of energy. Round about were other 'presences' in a circle of compassion and understanding.

'You can't come yet,' she was told. 'Not now. There is work for you to do.' And she was given specific instructions.

'Instructions?' Jeremy prompted again.

Toni went on to speak of the work she had since been doing as a result of what she had been told – researching and communicating with others about health risks posed by developments in modern society. She spoke as one supercharged with energy and conviction.

The conversation ended with Toni emerging from the chook pen and giving Jeremy a hug, laughing still.

Jeremy went next door to find no one at home.

Nevertheless, he drove home in heightened mood. 'There are more things in heaven and earth …' he said to himself.

Somehow, his encounter with Toni had enlarged his sympathies, while, at the same time, he felt he had encouraged Toni in her very different pursuit of truth.

The next Sunday, Jeremy spoke with unusual directness. There are many pathways to God, he told his people, and there are many different ways of being assured of God's presence with us.

'We come from God, we belong to God, we go to God,' he said, quoting St Augustine, 'but in that journey, we may follow very different paths. But be assured that our heavenly Father awaits us all.

'The glow of his presence and peace will surround us,' he concluded.

He smiled as he thought where those words came from.

Taking the Big Step

Josie tried to keep herself apart from parish matters, but with Jeremy's office being in the Vicarage, sometimes she couldn't help noticing things. 'We should have a separate entrance for the office,' she often said, but then, she'd counter-argue, perhaps it was good if she was able to keep just the smallest of fingers on the pulse of the parish.

On this particular evening, she couldn't help hearing the sobbing as Narelle was leaving.

Narelle was to be married to Peter the following Saturday, and Josie guessed what was the problem.

'Cold feet?' she murmured as Jeremy joined her in the kitchen.

'In a way,' replied Jeremy. 'But more than that. She's a firm believer that marriages are for ever, and for ever seems such an eternity for her. It's the hugeness of marriage, not the man, that's causing the stage-fright.'

'Is she in love?' asked Josie.

Jeremy paused. 'Yes, I believe she's in love.'

'So would I be,' teased Josie. 'With that Peter!'

'Mmm,' said Jeremy. Josie had the knack of sometimes putting him off balance. 'The wedding is in real doubt,' he continued, 'but she's coming back tomorrow night. She'll have to make her decision then. It can't be left any longer.'

'Mmm.' It was Josie this time. Jeremy wondered at her tone, but said nothing.

The marriage of Narelle and Peter was a marriage of the old kind. It was the first time for years Jeremy had written separate addresses for a couple in the Marriage Register.

It so chanced that as Narelle was leaving work for her lunch break the next day, Josie was passing in the street. 'Fancy meeting you!' said Josie.

Twenty minutes later, they were up to their second cup in the Delightful Grounds coffee shop. 'Thirty-five years,' Josie was saying.

Narelle listened in some sort of amazement. 'That's my whole life one and a half times over! You've been married all that time! How could you do it?!'

'I just took a punt on it,' said Josie. 'All life's a sort of punt, really. Everything that happens is a mixture of what we plan and what just comes along by accident.' She paused. 'And you can throw a bit of God's planning into the mixture.'

Narelle was drinking it all in.

'I believe in letting the big things in life happen just as they come,' Josie went on. 'Then work like fury to make them succeed.'

'And marriage?' asked Narelle.

'Then you've got two people working like fury to make it succeed. That's the real adventure of marriage,' Josie replied.

'An adventure?' repeated Narelle, wondering.

Ten minutes later, you might have seen the two women leaving the shop, hugging fervently, then going their separate ways.

'That was Narelle on the phone,' said Jeremy, coming in from his office. 'Said there was no need to come tonight, and everything's hunky-dory for Saturday. She sounded very happy. Something must have got into her.'

'I wonder what's happened,' muttered Josie, as she stirred the soup.

'Mmm,' said Jeremy, stroking his chin.

The Valley of the Shadow

At seven o'clock each morning it was Father Jeremy's practice to slip across to the church and say the Daily Office. Mostly he was there alone. Sometimes others joined him. Chloe came some Friday mornings. Others would come for a while, but then tailed off when winter came. Jeremy didn't mind. He rather enjoyed the stillness of being alone. Now and then he played a little game and imagined someone was with him. He would say their responses for them in a different voice.

Imagine his surprise one Monday morning when Brian Burleigh bustled in just after he had started. Brian was an irregular member of the congregation and had never appeared here before. He seemed to be in some distress.

'Sorry to interrupt,' he began. 'We've had bad news. The wife has been up all night.' It looked to Jeremy that Brian had also been up all night.

'It's the daughter,' Brian went on. He found it hard to say the words, but eventually continued, 'Elise. She's thirty-six. Two kids. They told her yesterday.'

Brian's eyes watered and he stopped, to control himself.

'A bad diagnosis?' Jeremy murmured, after a time.

'No hope,' Brian continued. 'Three months, they say.'

There was a different kind of quietness now. Jeremy leaned forward and took Brian's hand. After a minute or two, Brian sat up straight. His tone changed.

'I can't understand, Vicar,' he said. 'That's why I've come. How can it happen? To a girl like Elise? Did we have her and rear her just for this? And others depending on her.'

Jeremy waited. 'How can God do this?' Brian went on. 'How can he let this happen? Can you tell me?' Brian's voice was rising, accusing.

Again Jeremy waited. Logical arguments spun through his head. Passages of scripture, too. Jesus never promised that God would prevent bad things happening, he thought. People get the wrong idea of God in Sunday School and never grow out of it. But he pushed these ideas away.

'Can you remember when Elise was a little girl, when she was baptised, perhaps,' Jeremy said. He waited. 'God was with her then,' he went on. 'Do you remember her as a growing girl? Do you remember her on her wedding day? God was with her then.' Jeremy paused. Brian's shoulders were slumped, his head sinking, half listening, half lost to Jeremy's words. 'Do you remember when Elise had her little ones?' he went on. 'God was with her.'

Jeremy waited for a long time. 'God has always been with Elise. He is now. He always will be,' then, in an undertone, 'just as he was when Jesus was on the cross. He is Elise's heavenly Father. He will be with her now and in the future and for all time.'

There was no more said. After a minute or two, Brian muttered a thank-you and hurried away.

Jeremy was strangely quiet over breakfast. Josie left him alone. 'It will come out soon enough,' she said to herself.

High Stakes

The phone rang unusually early, when it was barely light.

The caller was too excited to give a name. 'Jeremy, you'd better have a look at the front of the church,' he said, and hung up with what Jeremy thought was something of a snigger. He bounded out of bed. 'Vandals again!' he muttered to Josie, as he dragged a tracksuit on.

Despite the early hour, a small crowd had gathered in the street looking up at the church tower. St Michael's was an old bluestone church, with a square tower at the western end, the street end. A solid stone wall rose from street level to the top of the crenelated tower ten metres above. From the top of the tower, suspended by ropes, hung a large grey woollen blanket, with the words, 'SAVE THE PLANET' crudely daubed across it in red paint.

Most of the people were also sniggering, and Jeremy himself couldn't stop smiling. But how was it done? Who could have done it? Quite a few of the congregation had an activist outlook on global warming, but they were too elderly – and staid - to have performed this feat. Besides, the stairway to the tower was kept locked.

As the day wore on, the explanation came to light. A police car arrived with Lenny and Jerry, two thirteen-year-old boys, in the back seat. Jeremy recognised Lenny from Sunday School some years earlier. He in particular seemed shamefaced by being brought to face the Vicar. They were hauled into Jeremy's study, the policeman standing alongside, while the confession was made.

Jeremy's interest was on the technical side. How had they done it? 'Easy,' said Lenny. 'You shouldn't keep the key under that brick.' They'd prepared the blanket the night before in Jerry's father's shed, carried it through the street in the dark, got into the tower, wrapped a brick in each bottom corner of the blanket to make it hang properly, roped the blanket to the parapet, and made their escape.

'Why?' asked Jeremy. 'Why did you do it?'

'We're doing climate change at school, and we wanted to do something to wake the town up,' said Lenny.

The police officer volunteered that no action would be taken apart from an official warning, and "a telling-off from you, if you could."

'Leave them with me for a few minutes,' Jeremy said, and the policeman went through to the hallway outside.

'Congratulations!' said Jeremy as soon as they were left alone. 'The town does need waking up, and you've done it. It's the best thing that's happened here for a long time.'

'But I've got to go through the motions for our friend out there,' Jeremy went on, as he raised his voice. 'So never let me catch you interfering with church property again, do you hear! You won't get off so lightly next time!'

Just before he opened the door to deliver the boys back to a smug-looking policeman, Jeremy slipped a ten-dollar note into each boy's shirt pocket. 'Well done!' he whispered. 'We'll leave your sign there all week.'

Out of the Mouths of Babes

All was still. It was at that momentary pause before the Confession that Danny entered the church. The creak of the door turned all heads towards the entrance as Danny stumbled into the worship area. He was dressed in the typical gear of a down-and-outer. His unshaven face and wild hair added to the impression.

Danny slumped down on the front seat close to where he had come in. The congregation themselves stumbled through the words of the Confession, though it was obvious that all minds were on the unexpected visitor. A frisson of expectation swept through the people: "Now we have a chance to practise our Christian compassion and forbearance," was the unspoken, but dominating feeling. If only he had realised it, Danny was, at that moment, everybody's darling.

For the next fifteen minutes, Danny variously slept, hiccupped, and muttered unintelligibly to himself. As Father Jeremy stepped up to the lectern for his sermon, he was praying fervently for Danny to go quietly to sleep. All was well for a few minutes, and Jeremy began to relax. But then, to everybody's horror, Danny rose from his seat and walked with some deliberation towards the lectern. He stood beside Jeremy.

Jeremy paused and turned to the intruder. He noticed that Danny's eyes were fixed firmly on the microphone.

'Would you like to say something to us?' he asked, taking the bull by the horns.

After an eternity of deliberation, Danny said, 'Yes.'

Jeremy ushered him to the stand and, in his turn, stood warily at Danny's side. The people were on tenterhooks.

Danny cleared his throat, looked up, then burst out, 'Hallelujah!'

The congregation took a moment to take this in, then burst into resounding applause.

Danny turned to Jeremy, but remained where he was. 'Is there anything else you want to say?' asked Jeremy, encouragingly.

Danny did not reply, and Jeremy prompted him. 'Thanks for the 'Hallelujah' you gave us. Is there a reason you said that?'

Danny stared at the clergyman as if a gigantic struggle of memory was going on inside him. He turned to the microphone. 'Because …,' he began, 'because …,' then, in a rush, 'because God so loved the world that he gave his only-begotten Son that everyone who believed in him should not perish, but have everlasting life. John 3:16.'

Here, Danny stopped abruptly, stared down at his toes and took a step backwards. Jeremy abandoned the rest of his sermon. 'That's preaching enough for anyone,' he said, and moved on to the Creed.

Danny stood for a moment, then sauntered to the back of the church where he remained quietly for the rest of the service.

Afterwards, as Danny was leaving, Jeremy shook his hand. 'You know your Bible!' he remarked.

Danny looked deep into Jeremy's eyes and said, 'Well, my dad was a minister, you know.'

Jeremy threw his arms around the young man, then, as Danny turned to go, he said, simply, 'Come again, won't you.'

A Lady of Ample Proportions

The annual meeting of the Ladies Guild had ended. As usual, Father Jeremy was asked to celebrate the Eucharist, then the business was conducted with Jeremy in the chair. Afterwards there was a splendid afternoon tea.

Jeremy was on the point of leaving, actually making towards the door, when Flora waved shyly to him. He stopped.

'I'm sorry to bother you with this, Father.' Flora, in her simple way, was one of the few of the regulars who called him 'Father'. 'You may think this is silly,' and here Flora dropped her voice almost to a whisper, 'but I'm really worried about my weight.'

Jeremy's eyebrows moved upward just a fraction. It was true, not to put too fine a point on it, that Flora was a lady of ample proportions. Jeremy wondered how on earth he could help.

'At the Christian Women Together meeting on Monday night, they said I should pray about it,' Flora went on. 'Would it be right to pray about something like that?'

Jeremy pondered the matter for a moment. Flora looked at him with trusting eyes.

Suddenly, an idea dawned on Jeremy. 'Flora,' he beamed, 'drop in to the Vicarage tomorrow morning, could you? We can talk more about it then.'

Early the next morning, Jeremy could be seen hunting amongst the old magazines in the Op Shop. He soon found what he was looking for and bore the journal home.

'Flora,' he began when his visitor arrived the following morning, 'I've been thinking. I don't believe you should ask God for help with a personal matter like this unless you were prepared to submit yourself to some spiritual or physical discipline as a sign of your good faith.

'Ash Wednesday is next week, and Lent is a good time to put your good intentions into practice.

'What I would like you to do is to pray every morning for the forty days of Lent that God would help you in your genuine desire to lose some weight. After all, the Bible tells us that the body is the temple of the spirit.'

Flora looked at him with eyes aglow.

'Meanwhile,' Jeremy continued, 'you undertake your plan of self-discipline. I want you to follow precisely the directions in this magazine. Here, I'll show you just where.'

Jeremy drew a thick red line around the dieting instructions listed there, and Flora left with a look of determination on her face.

Over the following weeks, each Sunday, Jeremy eyed Flora with increasing interest. Flora remained silent on the matter of her progress, but Jeremy thought he noticed a distinct change for the better.

On Easter morning, Flora could contain herself no longer. 'I've lost thirty pounds,' she declared as she filed out of church. 'Thirty pounds. In six weeks!'

Jeremy purred. 'It's amazing what God can achieve with the help of man,' he replied. 'Or woman,' he added.

'I can't wait to get to the Christian Women meeting to tell them about it,' Flora called as she hurried out the door.

The Deanery Meeting

To outward appearances, Father Jeremy was remarkably even-tempered.

Nothing seemed to perturb the steady pace and relaxed demeanour of his ways. His face bore the same quizzical and sympathetic expression, no matter what the situation.

Josie knew better, of course, though even she was surprised by the vehemence of Jeremy's language that afternoon.

Jeremy had just returned from the Deanery meeting. His colleagues gathered every two months for an hour or two to eat lunch together and to exchange news and views. Jeremy attended these meetings rather as a matter of duty.

Occasionally there was a speaker, and on this occasion a young priest from the neighbouring Deanery had 'given a paper' as he described it.

'That man!' Jeremy expostulated. 'That man!' he repeated.

Josie waited.

'Personal health and safety!' burst out Jeremy.

'We have to look after ourselves. That's what it's all about,' he went on, a little more consecutively.

'I'm too old,' Jeremy groaned as he sank deeply into his chair. 'If that's the church, it's time I was out of it.'

After a comforting cup of tea – and one of Josie's special shortbreads – Jeremy was able to give Josie something of what the Bright Young Visitor had said.

It seemed that it was now vital to successful ministry to take the phone off the hook during meals, to receive visitors only by appointment, to live in a house some distance from the church, and to abstain from any contact with the parish during one's day off.

'Visiting! Not one word about visiting!' Jeremy said. 'It's all mechanical, ministry. It's a science. Aim, Apparatus, Method,' he went on as a vague memory of his High School science experiments flashed into his mind.

'Work-life balance, he kept talking about. My work *is* my life,' Jeremy roared.

Jeremy's anger began to subside. 'Just as well Fred wasn't there,' he went on. Fred Naismith was Jeremy's close companion. They'd studied together in their early days. Now they worked in nearby parishes. 'Fred would have stood up and said something,' Jeremy said. 'Would have been a scene, but, of, course, we were all too polite.'

Eventually, Jeremy's ire softened. A second cup of tea and a second shortbread did their work.

When the phone rang, Josie noted the alacrity with which Jeremy sprang to answer it.

'I'll have to go,' Jeremy said as he took up the car keys. 'Alison's not too good.'

During Jeremy's absence, Josie put the finishing touches to her recovery scheme.

When Jeremy returned, she had the evening meal ready for the table, and a glass of red wine beside each of their places.

'I had a peep at your diary,' she said as she was dishing up. 'You've got nothing down for Friday night, I see.'

Jeremy saw something was coming.

'So I thought we might have someone here for dinner.'

The idea hit just the right note. 'The Naismiths?' suggested Jeremy.

'I've already phoned them,' Josie replied. 'They're coming at seven o'clock.'

Brothers Living Together in Unity

Father Jeremy had been in the Parish of St Michael's for five years, and he had good reason to think the parish was in good heart. He wouldn't have used that phrase. Indeed, he wouldn't have allowed himself to think that thought. He was aware of one or two little niggles, not concerning himself, but between people within the congregation … and they did concern him as the pastor of the community.

Guy and Chris seemed to get under one another's skin. No particular incident had occurred to cause this rift – or none that Jeremy was aware of – and that made it harder to deal with. Both came to the ten o'clock service with their wives, but kept well apart. Everybody in the congregation understood the situation.

'I should do something about it,' Jeremy said to Josie. 'I don't like to bring them together to talk about it. It should come from them.'

The quarterly Men's Breakfast was due the following month. Jeremy wondered if this would give him an opportunity …

It was the custom, after the meal, for Jeremy to read a Bible passage and give a short homily based on it – just a few minutes.

Jeremy rose and glanced around the tables, observing Guy and Chris widely separated as usual.

'I'll take Psalm 133 for our reading,' he began:

> *Behold how good and how lovely it is:*
>
> *When brothers live together in unity ...*
>
> *It is like a dew of Hermon:*
>
> *Like the dew that falls upon the hill of Zion.*

Jeremy put the book down.

He spoke a little about his childhood when his brother and he had quarrelled and niggled, but how they came to an age when they put this behind them and "lived together in unity".

'We are all children of God,' he went on, 'brothers in Christ. How vast is God's love for us and how petty our divisions and misunderstandings when considered in the light of God's overwhelming love for each one of us and Christ's giving of himself for every single one.'

Jeremy spoke with unusual fervor. A heightened feeling was palpable throughout the room. Jeremy closed his brief address. His eyes were cast down severely upon the table. The meal wound up amidst a low murmur of conversation.

The men stood, pushed in their chairs, took up their coats, and began to move out towards the street in small clusters of particular companions.

Jeremy dared to look up. His heart leapt. Guy and Chris were walking side by side amongst a small gaggle of men. He looked away quickly as though the mere sight of them could destroy the feeling within him.

'How was the Breakfast?' enquired Josie.

'The porridge was very good, the toast fine, the tea excellent,' he replied.

'You're holding something back,' Josie probed.

'Well, the Vicar gave a short talk. We'll have to wait and see how that went down, but the signs are good.'

Josie stood, wondering.

Father Jeremy Swaps Pulpits

Father Jeremy was not renowned for his preaching

He prepared carefully, though the sources of his preparation, his books from theological college, were now rather dated.

That was of little moment to his congregation, but the fact that the books and passages consulted were the same year after year meant that his listeners tended to get the same message year after year.

Still, no one complained. They loved Father Jeremy not for his eloquence, but for himself.

One morning Father Jeremy was surprised to receive a phone call from the Vicar of a distant parish asking if a pulpit swap could be arranged.

It seemed that the enquiring Vicar had grown up in St Michael's Parish and he would dearly love to return to the place of his nurturing, presumably, thought Father Jeremy, in order to demonstrate his superlative preaching skills.

A cloud came over the poor man's face. Two things worried him, one that his own inadequacies would be thoroughly revealed to his people by this upstart, and, secondly, that the same inadequacies would be painfully revealed to the swap parish.

However, Father Jeremy could think of no valid reason not to consent, not on the phone at any rate, so it was agreed, and the date set, a month away.

There was little to report from Father Jeremy's end. His two services went off without remark, although Jeremy was a little nettled to find a rather larger attendance than he was used to. The congregations seemed interested in William Barclay's sentiments about the Matthew passage, distilled, as they were, through the mind and pen of Jeremy. In the vestry afterwards, the Vicar's Warden thanked him for coming. 'It was nice to have a comfortable service,' he said. Jeremy wondered what he meant.

At home once more, Jeremy was anxious to hear how the visitor had performed, though he was restrained enough not to ask. It wasn't until the following Sunday that he had any inkling.

The eight-o'clockers hugged him one by one as they arrived. 'So glad you're back,' was the universal sentiment.

At ten, people were more forthright. Through the chorus of comments, Jeremy gathered (a) that the sermon had lasted for forty minutes, (b) that the preacher had left the pulpit and paced up and down, severely embarrassing those seated in the front pews, and (c) that his sermon had ended with an altar call, which fell on deaf ears. There had been no response.

At the Parish Council meeting on the Wednesday following, there was an unusual warmth of feeling around the table. At the end, apropos of nothing at all, the Rector's Warden moved a vote of appreciation to Father Jeremy for "his loving care of his people and his faithful conduct of the Sunday services". Passed with acclamation.

At home, Josie said much the same thing, but in her own way.

'I don't think we'll be going in search of foreign pulpits in the near future,' she declared.

'Perhaps you're right,' Jeremy replied.

A Bad Hair Day

The early service was fine, but then, there's not much that can go wrong – no singing, no fuss, just the liturgy and Holy Communion. And the congregation were all regulars who knew the service as well as Father Jeremy did.

But at ten o'clock nothing at all went right. It started when the organist played the wrong tune for the first hymn – '*St Columba*' for 'The King of Love my Shepherd is' instead of '*Dominus Regit me*'. The people soon picked it up, but it left Jeremy feeling uneasy. He knew that bad things come in bunches.

Next, the lay reader read the wrong lesson for the epistle. There were alternative readings given in the lectionary, so it was understandable. The trouble was that Jeremy had based his sermon on the other alternative, so the sermon became something of a shambles, or so it seemed to Jeremy.

Still full of self-reproach, his mind went blank at the altar rail when he was giving the bread in the Communion, and he couldn't think of Dawn Jenkins's Christian name. He'd tried to cover it up by not using Christian names for the rest of the row, but he felt that Dawn had realised what he was doing.

To cap the whole morning off, at the end of the service he'd forgotten to get the congregation to sing Happy Birthday for Frank Simmons. Frank was the Grand Old Man of the parish, and a grumpy one to boot. To make it up, Jeremy had broken in to everyone's morning tea afterwards – which he hated doing - and had them sing for Frank then. But he couldn't help noticing the scowl on Frank's face.

At lunch, Josie noticed Jeremy was in a bad mood. He'd thrown his books down in his study; he said not a word to her; he began eating without saying grace.

'What's up?' she enquired.

'Everything,' replied Jeremy. 'The service. Couldn't you see? Everything went wrong.'

Josie was silent for a space. Then, 'Did anything go right?' she asked gently.

'Nothing!' said Jeremy.

Another silence.

'Well, I've been counting up the things that *did* go right,' Josie began.

Jeremy raised his head just a little.

'I'll tell you,' Josie went on. 'The people had the Bible read to them; they sang four good hymns; they prayed together; they said their confession and you gave them a prayer of forgiveness; they came up for their Communion … and they all had a jolly good time together.'

'Hmm,' said Jeremy, but he remained quiet for the rest of the meal.

When Jeremy returned from the hospital later that afternoon, Josie presented him with a beautiful chocolate cake. 'Dawn Jenkins brought it round,' she told him. "She said she'd been thinking about that bit in this morning's readings about loving one another with mutual affection, and she'd made the cake to show you how much everyone loved you.'

Jeremy smiled a deep smile.

'So everything's all right, then?' asked Josie.

The Day Off

It was after tea on Sunday, and Father Jeremy's thoughts went to the next day. So did Josie's. She looked across the table. She knew Monday was Jeremy's day off, but she knew how often things in the parish cropped up on Mondays, and somehow the day became like every other day for Jeremy - and for her as well.

'Tomorrow?' she began.

Jeremy shook his head. 'There's so much paperwork to catch up on. And I really should see old Alec. The ward sister says he hasn't much time left.'

Josie waited a few moments. 'Isn't there something in the Bible about having a day off?'

'Not that I can recall,' replied Jeremy, cautiously. He had fallen into his wife's traps too often not to recognise a danger signal in what she had just said. And he was always nervous when someone asked about something in the Bible. What if Josie should know more than he did!

'Actually, it's somewhere in Genesis that I'm thinking of,' Josie continued. 'I'll look it up now,' and she disappeared in the direction of Jeremy's study.

Jeremy sank back in his chair. He had an inkling of what was coming.

Josie returned, thumbing through a copy of the Bible. Jeremy smiled to himself.

'Here it is,' said Josie, and she read, a note of superiority in her voice, 'Genesis, chapter 2. "And on the seventh day God finished the work that he had done, and he rested on the seventh day from all the work that he had done."

'Now if it's good enough for God to take one day a week off, then it's good enough for you,' concluded Josie.

'I'm flattered that you put me on the same level as God,' said Jeremy, 'but I can't accept the honour. Besides everything that God did was perfect and there was nothing left to be tidied up afterwards. I've got a lot of things to be tidied-up after this past week.'

'Oh well, I'll just have to go by myself then,' said Josie, with an air of finality.

Josie's words hit the target. Jeremy raised his eyebrows. 'Where?' he asked uncomfortably.

'I thought of going to the Rocky Horror Show in town,' she said as she began to gather up the dishes.

Jeremy burst into a roar of laughter.

'You! The Rocky Horror Show!' he gasped.

But by then Josie had come and put her arm around her husband. 'I was sure you would want to come too,' she grinned.

Jeremy defences were hopelessly down.

So it was that the next morning, Jeremy and Josie were seen walking to the station to catch the 8.40 into town. The National Gallery lay ahead of them, then lunch at Sophie's favourite dining place, and that new French film in the afternoon.

And of course, Josie had rung the hospital. Old Alec was doing fine.

Unwanted Gifts

'There's a strange man walking up the path,' said Josie. 'And a very large car parked in the street.' Her chair at the lunch table was strategically placed for just such a situation. Her warning gave Father Jeremy enough time to put on his clerical collar before he opened the door.

The face was unfamiliar to Jeremy. But, with a hearty handshake, the visitor stepped inside. 'Remember me?' he blurted out.

Father Jeremy did not remember him, but was quickly supplied with his deficiency. 'Bruce Wilton,' he exclaimed. 'You saw me in the hospital last month. When I was waiting for those test results.'

Jeremy's memory was stirred. 'I'm sorry,' he offered. 'You look rather different now.'

Bruce Wilton was a business man from a place further down the line. He had received a possibly serious preliminary diagnosis and had been admitted to the hospital for further tests. He'd demanded the nursing staff send for a priest. 'Sky-pilot' was actually the term he used.

Jeremy had entered the room to find a pasty-faced, anxious, but nevertheless blustering figure – Bruce Wilton.

The patient wasted no time. 'It may be bad news, Padre,' he had begun. 'Really bad news. I want you to pray for me. You're the professional,' he added with a weak grin. 'I've got five thousand dollars for you if you can pull me through,' he went on.

Jeremy tried to hide his look of disdain, but said nothing. He'd heard that sort of talk before. After a moment, he took the man's hand and after saying the Lord's Prayer, prayed that the patient would receive God's comfort and encouragement, and if it be God's will, be restored to health. A short time later he left his visiting card by the bedside and departed.

Now he was face-to face once more with his would-be benefactor.

In the study, Mr Wilton took a chequebook from his inside pocket, and said, 'Well, I'm a man of my word. You got me through. The test results were clear, and I'm here to give you your reward. Five thousand, wasn't it?'

Father Jeremy held out a restraining hand. 'Just a moment,' he said gently. 'It's not *my* reward. If there's been healing, it comes from God, not from me. And God doesn't have a bank account, you know,' he added with a smile.

Bruce Wilton looked puzzled. 'For the church, then,' he said weakly.

'Sorry to disappoint you again,' Jeremy replied. 'The church isn't like a gun for hire. You asked for our help and we gave it, freely and willingly. That's what we do.'

The man looked confused. He shook his head.

'Then? … ' he began.

'Nothing else,' said Jeremy, as he ushered the man out the front door. 'But the Food Relief Centre needs a lot of help. They're just across from the railway station.'

'What was all that about?' enquired Josie, when Jeremy returned.

'Just a small misunderstanding,' Jeremy said, as picked up his cold cup of tea.

A Warm Feeling for Mother Church

Now Father Jeremy was not against women priests. He had been once, but that was before the Rev Angela Thurston had come to be Vicar of his neighbouring parish. She had completely won him over, partly because she was such a good priest, but also because she obviously liked him. 'She likes everybody,' Jeremy thought to himself, 'but it's nice that she likes me.'

These days, Jeremy was a committed supporter of the ordination of women. He hadn't studied the pros and cons to any depth; it was just that he couldn't think of any reasons against it. And the Rev Angela liked him. That was enough.

So it was with a troubled mind that he turned to the matter of Sheila McKerras. Sheila had been studying theology by distance education for several years. They hadn't talked much about it. Jeremy was always nervous about discussing theology. But then he hadn't seen Sheila very often to talk about anything. Sheila was an occasional church attender. Jeremy sometimes wondered if she went to another church. Another denomination, perhaps. When she did come, she took up a vaguely dissatisfied stance. Why are some people like that? he wondered.

Now, to make things doubly difficult for him, Sheila had come to ask for his backing in her application for ordination. She was to see the Bishop the following week, and would like him to write a letter of support to take with her. His instinct was to say no, he couldn't write such a letter. But then, would he be accused of being sexist? You had to tread carefully in these things nowadays. Some people were very prickly about these things.

But why did he feel like this? Jeremy needed some kind of reasoned support. After Sheila had gone, Jeremy looked up an old Ad Clerum the Bishop had written about applicants for ordination. There was one particular phrase the Bishop had used that he couldn't quite remember. Jeremy glanced down the list of desirable attributes. They had to do with things like personal qualities and a sense of vocation and a firm faith. But, no, there was something else. Something that had struck a chord in Jeremy's mind.

There it was. In his final paragraph, the Bishop had written about an ordinand having "a warm feeling for Mother Church". You could measure many things about a person. You could perhaps measure their personal qualities, even their sense of vocation, perhaps their faith. But a "warm feeling for Mother Church", this you couldn't measure. Yet this is precisely why it appealed to Jeremy. His instinct told him that his instinct was correct. This is what worried him about Sheila McKerras. Where was her warm feeling for Mother Church?

Jeremy went to his writing desk. "Dear Sheila," he began, "Thank you for coming to see me about your application for ordination. I wish you well in your interview with the Bishop, but at this stage I don't feel I can write the letter you asked me for …"

Inter-Church Relations

Father Jeremy and Father Gregory were good friends.

Gregory Mainz was Rector of St Joseph's some blocks away. The two had come to know each other through the Ministers' Association, and they often crossed paths on occasions like Anzac Day and the High School Speech Night.

A polite recognition of each other's work had grown into a warm feeling of fellowship. Father Gregory had preached at the recent ecumenical service at St Michael's.

Now Gregory was on the phone asking Jeremy if he would come to a function at the Catholic Secondary College. Their new chapel was to be officially opened by the Bishop, and it would be nice, Gregory said, if Jeremy could represent the local churches and perhaps read one of the Bible readings.

Jeremy was delighted. He could show his genuine respect for his fellow-religionists with very little bother for himself.

The service went off splendidly. Jeremy read well, and he felt very comfortable sitting with the Bishop and other

Catholic clergy in the sanctuary. 'How nice not to be in charge for a change,' he thought.

Afterwards, when the Bishop had left and the attendees dispersed, Gregory whispered to Jeremy, 'We're having a drink in the presbytery. You'd better come.'

There were six or seven of the local priests there.

Jeremy was greatly honoured. He was the centre of conversation. The others seemed to hang on his words. His Irish background was the subject of much laughter. Tales were told of the twists and turns of family life that had led each of them into the Catholic Church or, in Jeremy's case, into the Anglican Church.

Several bottles of excellent red wine were consumed, a special bottling, Jeremy noticed. The housekeeper had left a rich fruit cake. There was an easiness of companionship amongst them all that Jeremy found particularly warming. Each man seemed perfectly content within himself and perfectly at ease with the others. 'I could almost become a Catholic,' he said to himself.

As he drove home, Jeremy pondered where the spirit of good fellowship came from. Because all of them were men, he wondered? Or that they were unmarried, the others, at any rate? Or that they were freed from the usual constraints whilst amongst lay people? Or was it a genuine expression of Christian love? Or all these combined?

His mind was full of these things as he walked into the Rectory.

Without forethought, he wrapped Josie into a bear-hug embrace.

Josie noticed the slight aroma of red wine, but the glow on Jeremy's face was not just the glow of that stimulation.

'So you've had a good night,' she said at last.

'They've got something, those Catholics,' he replied

Josie stayed silent.

'I think I'll start a new movement,' Jeremy said. 'The Anglo-Catholic Society for Mutual Goodwill – the *ACSMG*. It sounds good!'

'I think it already exists,' Josie countered, 'if you look up your Diocesan handbook. Besides,' she said with a grin, 'you've never started anything in your life!'

Jeremy chased her out of the room.

The Accident

The team at the funeral parlour were old friends of Father Jeremy. They always made sure to check his availability before arranging a funeral. They'd send him full details of the family. They kept in touch before and often after each funeral. And they offered him a lift in the hearse if the service was to be at the Crematorium.

That was easier in the old days when the hearses had bench seats, and all three could fit in – the funeral director, his assistant, and Jeremy. The fourth passenger would ride in the back. On the way home, with the solemnity of the service completed, there was usually a good deal of light-hearted conversation.

It was on such an occasion, as the hearse was being driven home, that a motorcyclist came out from a slip road and drove into the side of the hearse. It was a glancing collision rather than full-on. The bike fell crumpled and steaming on the roadside, and the rider lay on his back beside it, silent and still.

The hearse, only slightly knocked off-course, pulled up on the roadside and the three occupants rushed to the aid of the rider. His helmet had fallen off and they could see he was a young man, lightly bearded, and that there were no obvious signs of injury. He lay there breathing steadily, but deeply unconscious.

The three bent over him in concern. Just then the young man's eyes opened. He looked up to see a priest and two funeral directors leaning over him, and promptly relapsed into unconsciousness.

Within a few minutes, several cars had stopped and a small group of people had gathered. An ambulance arrived, and a police car as well. The ambulance officers attended to the injured man, while the police officers took down the details they needed. Father Jeremy was relieved to see the bike-rider, apparently having regained full consciousness and without serious injuries, being placed in the ambulance. 'They'll probably keep him for observation,' one of the paramedics said before the ambulance headed off to the hospital. Jeremy waved what he hoped was an encouraging farewell to the young man, while the police attended to the bike and cleared the scene. The hearse was only slightly damaged, and the three men continued their journey.

The next morning, early, Father Jeremy called at the hospital, to find the young man – another Jeremy – waiting for some test results before being allowed home. He was rather subdued in spirit, but cheerful.

'I can't remember the accident itself,' he said. 'The first thing I remember was waking up and seeing you three looking down at me. I thought my time had come!'

Jeremy didn't stay long. He found his new friend to be an apprentice plumber, who'd been riding home from work when the crash occurred. Jeremy left his card. 'If there's anything I can ever do for you, please get in touch.'

The other Jeremy smiled and reached out his hand. 'Thanks a lot,' he said. 'You never know.'

Strange Meeting

Father Jeremy decided to walk to the Morrisons. It was a fine morning, and he could call on one or two others on the way home. It was good to walk, he decided. There was something old-fashioned and comfortable about the Vicar walking to visit his flock. Like the village constable on the beat, he smiled to himself.

His walk took him through the Park. He'd noticed one of the workmen there once or twice before, an older man, almost too old for that sort of work, Jeremy thought. Today, the man was weeding a bed alongside the path, and Jeremy stopped to talk.

He'd worked on the Council staff for some years, Stan (for that was his name) told Jeremy, since he'd come down from the bush. Now he lived quite close by. He spoke slowly and respectfully. Father Jeremy warmed to his companion. He was a genuine man of the soil. He spoke of his work in the Park with affection, as if he was working his own land. Jeremy listened with warm interest. After they'd engaged in some mutual weather-forecasting, Stan appeared to notice Jeremy's clerical collar for the first time.

'You'd be that Father Jeremy from St Michael's,' he said, slowly.

Jeremy confessed that it was indeed he.

'I've heard about you,' said Stan. Jeremy often heard those words, never without some discomfort. What might actually have been said? he always thought. Stan went on. 'I was past your church once when they were singing this hymn.'

Jeremy waited. He could see there was more that Stan wanted to say.

'Yes,' the old man went on. 'I stood and listened for a while. It was … lovely.'

That word, 'lovely', didn't come easily to this old man of the land. There was another pause. 'Did you never get to any church, then?' Jeremy asked gently.

'Never could. I never could,' Stan returned, with some fire. 'Was never christened, you see. I come from up north, there. Miles from anywhere. There was no one to do the job.'

Jeremy's eyes softened. He waited. This was a conversation Stan had waited perhaps all his life to happen.

'Would you like to be christened?' Jeremy asked softly. The old man looked up eagerly.

Jeremy hesitated, not sure what he was going to say. 'Have you thought about God?' he asked rather awkwardly. 'He's here,' Stan said. He spread out his hands and looked around him.

'And Jesus …' Jeremy went on, not sure how to finish the sentence.

'I speak to him all the time.'

There were one or two others in the Park. They stopped to witness an amazing sight. A man in black taking some water from a nearby tap. An aged figure standing with bowed head. And they might have heard the words, 'I baptise you in the name of the Father and of the Son and of the Holy Spirit'.

Jeremy went to leave. 'Give me your address,' he said. I'll talk to the Morrisons about giving you a lift next Sunday.'

The old man waved a farewell.

Families Disunited

The old woman had died, and the family had asked for a Christian funeral. The name rang a bell for Jeremy, and, after searching, he found it in an out-of-date parish roll: Emily Roylston, 14 Alexander Street. Years before his time she had come to church, it seemed, but now she had drifted beyond the church's knowledge and care.

 But the children remembered, and now, as he sat with them, he delighted in their insistence that their mother have "a good old Church of England funeral".

They talked about their mother's life, and Jeremy asked about the family.

A silence fell. There had been a rift many years ago.

It was an old story. Father Jeremy had heard it many times before.

Carol and her husband, Rex, had fallen out with the family over the division of spoils when Mr Roylston had died seven years earlier and had not spoken to any of them, including their mother, Emily, since then.

'Do you think they will come to the funeral?' Jeremy enquired.

There was a shaking of heads all round.

'I rang them when Mum died,' Roy, the oldest son, said, weakly. 'They listened, but put the phone down pretty quick.'

The conversation went on to other things. Jeremy's suggestions as to the readings and hymns were taken up readily. They would like 'Time to say Goodbye' – "you know, Andrea Bocelli and Sarah Brightman" at the end, and the St Kilda Football Club theme song at the graveside.

Jeremy smiled. He'd heard that many times before, also. He made a note in his notepad.

At the door, Jeremy turned to Roy, 'Perhaps you could speak to Carol again?'

Roy looked glum, but promised he'd try.

At home, Jeremy had an idea. He dug out the old church registers.

'Ah!' he muttered. Carol Joy Roylston, baptized, St Michael's, aged five months.

Spurred on, Jeremy searched further. The Confirmation register. There it was. Carol J Roylston. Confirmed by Bishop Strachan, St Michael's, aged thirteen.

'Isn't it sad!' said Josie over tea that night. 'Christmas the worst time for family bust-ups, and funerals the second worst.

'When we need each other most, we fly at each other's throats,' Josie went on.

'Don't despair,' Jeremy replied. 'There's a seed of forgiveness inside all of us.'

'And redemption,' added Josie.

The next day Jeremy dropped in on Carol and Rex. There was a red Toyota parked in the carport. He didn't get inside the house, but they talked freely to him. The word 'family' was mentioned quite a lot, and 'forgiveness on both sides' once or twice. Carol did most of the talking and Jeremy most of the listening. He thought he saw good signs in Rex's face. As he left, Jeremy told Carol how good it was to meet up with one of St Michael's 'old girls'.

'It's in other hands, now,' Jeremy said to Josie when he got home. 'Bigger hands than ours.'

On the appointed day, the family cars began to arrive.

Jeremy seemed abstracted. He was looking anxiously for a red Toyota.

Naughty Vicar

'I'm just waiting on your reflection'.

It was Margaret from the church office on the phone. Margaret came in on Wednesdays and Thursdays to type up the Sunday pew sheet and attend to the sundry things in the parish that had not been done, but which ought to have been done.

It was Jeremy's practice to write a few paragraphs by way of a reflection on the weekly readings. He'd write it on Wednesday evening and email it through to the church office for it to be ready for Margaret first thing Thursday morning. This week it had slipped his mind.

'I need to know how long it is so I can fit in all the other things,' Margaret went on. 'Your reflection, that is.'

For a moment, Jeremy's mind fixed on his reflection in the mirror he could see from where he stood. Thoughts of the Hall of Mirrors at Luna Park came into his head.

'Sorry, Margaret. I'll send it through as soon as I can. Give me half an hour.'

It was a rush job, and Jeremy barely looked it over before he clicked the 'Send' button, and thought no more about it.

Later in the day, across in the Office, he admired the neatly stacked pew sheets set out on the book trolley ready for Sunday morning.

'Thanks, Margaret,' he said, approvingly, as he went to leave. 'I'll be at the hospital for a while, then home, I expect.'

All was well for the rest of the week … but it was the calm before the storm!

'Naughty Vicar!' Tom Isles said, and shook his head, grinning. That was before the eight o'clock service.

Some joke had got round the congregation, Jeremy could tell. There were mutterings and smiles, but clearly an attempt to keep Jeremy out of the loop.

The same at ten o'clock. Afterwards, at the cup of tea, there were ribald comments at Jeremy's expense: 'Naughty, naughty, Jeremy,' Alice said, and Fred Counihan, the parish 'professor' called him 'our new moralist'. 'I'm not sure what the Bishop will say about this,' said someone else.

Finally, there was a joint decision to let Jeremy in on the banter.

'There!' Fred pulled out the pew sheet.

Jeremy raced through his reflection.

There, where he had meant to write, 'The whole sweep of the gospel calls us not to give way to our deep and unnatural urgings …', he had omitted the word 'not'.

And Margaret had pasted the unchecked copy straight into the pew sheet.

As Jeremy's eyes fell on the offending line and a horrified expression dawned on his face, everyone roared with laughter.

'We've all heard of the 'Naughty Bible,' Fred Counihan was saying. 'Now we've got our own 'Naughty Vicar'.

Worse was to come. Someone leaked the matter to the local paper ('I'm sure it was that wretch, Counihan!' Jeremy expostulated to Josie), and the following Wednesday, the front page banner headline echoed the sentiments of the parishioners.

'NAUGHTY VICAR', it proclaimed.

Father Jeremy's Clever Idea

Like most parish priests, Jeremy regarded the sermon as the main challenge of the Sunday morning service.

But to come up with fresh ideas Sunday after Sunday was not easy. Others might seem to find it easy, but not he.

Jeremy did keep his sermon notes from past years, and occasionally he dipped back into the past for inspiration. But he never felt comfortable doing that. Besides, there were one or two long-term members of the congregation who would utter snide remarks; 'Seemed to have heard something like that before, Vicar', or 'Old ideas never change, do they, Vicar!'

Whenever he was called 'Vicar', Jeremy knew there was a little barb wrapped up in the comment.

Then came his good idea. 'I'll give them something they can't complain about,' he said to Josie at Thursday lunch. Thursday was sermon preparation day.

'Yes, you'll see. This week I'll give them something straight from the horse's mouth.' His wife was left wondering.

Josie was listening with more than her usual concentration the following Sunday.

Jeremy's phrases did have a familiar sound, and they were striking, to say the least:

'Jesus of Nazareth,' Jeremy was saying, *'a man attested by God with deeds of power, wonders, and signs that God did through him – this man was handed over according to the definite plan and foreknowledge of God, was crucified and killed by the hands of those outside the law ...'*

'This doesn't sound like Jeremy,' thought Josie, as did quite a few in the congregation. Still Jeremy went on:

'But God raised him up, having freed him from death, because it was impossible for him to be held in its power.'

The service over, Jeremy had the distinct feeling that his sermon had not gone down well.

'Well, Vicar,' began Shirley Harris over the cup of tea, 'that sermon seemed to come from somewhere in the past.'

'The past!' added Max Long, who knew his New Testament, 'Straight out of the Acts of the Apostles! Peter's address at Pentecost, Acts, chapter 2.'

'Yes,' Jeremy replied. 'I thought you might like to hear Peter himself for a change. What more could you ask for?!'

Much discussion followed, the tenor of which was that Peter's words were all very well on the printed page, but Jeremy's words were more appropriate from the pulpit on a Sunday morning.

'Besides,' said old Mr McLean,' we don't come to church for the sermon, you know. Well, not just for the sermon.'

There was a chorus of agreement. 'It's everything,' said Jeremy's church warden, Jack. 'It's the whole thing –the Communion, the readings, the prayers - and the sermon.'

'And the hymns,' put in Sandra, the organist, a little sharply.

'And seeing everybody else,' added Julia.

Over lunch, Jeremy was in pensive mood. 'Perhaps I've worried a bit too much about my preaching,' he said.

Josie thought for some time, then replied, 'Perhaps we need Peter's thoughts and your words.'

Jeremy nodded. 'I'll have to think about that,' he said.

The New Car

It's true there were some problems with the car – the interior lights didn't work, there were scratches on the sides, a large dent in the rear caused anonymously in the supermarket car park, and a peculiar shudder in low gear that the garage men couldn't solve.

Still it was comfortable, reliable, and had never let them down. It was their own car. Jeremy didn't believe in having a diocesan car as part of his stipend package.

Josie was the agitator. 'We've had Old Faithful for ten years and you've got ten years to retirement,' she argued. 'You've got to have a new car some time. This one won't last for twenty years! Now is the perfect time.'

Jeremy was impressed by this logic. His trouble was what people would think when they saw him driving a brand spanking new car. 'There's a very sound argument,' he would say, 'that the Vicar should live the lifestyle of the average person in the parish. That's the whole theory of clergy stipends. We're not supposed to be either rich or poor. Just comfortable.'

'Pooh!' Josie replied. 'Lots of people have a new car. Why, the Andersons bought a BMW the other day. And what's the difference between having twenty thousand dollars in the Bank and spending twenty thousand dollars on a new car? It's the same money. People would understand that.'

Jeremy had to admit the force of this logic, also. But he still stalled.

One morning, he had a large smile on his face. 'I've decided what we can do about the car,' he said.

To Josie's anxious enquiries, he turned a deaf ear. 'You'll have to wait,' is all he would say.

The Annual General Meeting occurred the following Sunday, after the ten o'clock service. There was a large attendance, partly because of a mysterious agenda item. 'Vehicle' was all it said.

When the time came, Jeremy stood up and explained his situation. He repeated the arguments that had been canvassed over the Vicarage breakfast table. He spared nothing, to Josie's embarrassment, and finished by declaring that he wanted the meeting to decide the matter for him..

The discussion was brief and very one-sided. Speaker after speaker urged Jeremy to have a new vehicle. Jack, Jeremy's

Vicar's Warden, was the final speaker. 'I can't think of any Biblical reference that can help us, except perhaps that somewhere in the Old Testament it says that Jehu used to drive like a maniac. Let Jeremy not be the new Jehu, and have his new car,' he ended, to laughter.

'You clever thing,' Josie said later. 'You knew all along what people would say. Now you've got a new car and nipped all the criticism you were worried about in the bud at the same time. Two flies with one blow!'

Jeremy stoutly denied her accusation. 'I'm simply a poor parish priest, the servant of his people,' he said.

'Pooh' Josie said again, but added, 'I suppose we can allow our Vicar a little self-satisfaction.'

Jeremy had a quiet smile on his face.

Coming Back to Bite You

There was a long silence.

Both men were perfectly still, Jeremy sitting in front of his desk and, opposite him, his visitor who introduced himself simply as 'Alan'.

'Well, I'd better come to the point,' said the latter at last. 'This is not easy for me.'

Another pause. Then, 'I used to be in business here. It was a long time ago, and you wouldn't know anything about it.'

'That's all right,' said Jeremy. 'Maybe better that I don't.'

The man nodded. 'It was a good business. There were two of us in it. My partner did most of the front-of-house work, and I looked after the books and the ordering. Maybe you can see what's coming.'

More silence,

'We got on well,' Alan continued. 'We were friends. Still are, though we don't see each other that much now.

'We sold out in the end and went our own ways. We've both done well enough.'

Again Alan lapsed into silence. His eyes were fixed on the floor as though studying the pattern in the carpet.

'And?' said, Jeremy, finally.

'Well, I was fixing things. He never knew. With a bit of help from the suppliers and some simple jiggery-pokery, I siphoned off more than my share. Added up to about ten thousand dollars. Worth more now. Double that.'

Jeremy wanted to ease the man's difficulty in speaking of these things. 'So now you want to repay him,' he suggested.

Alan nodded.

'But you don't know how …', Jeremy went on.

'I couldn't face him. I really couldn't face him. He doesn't need it … God knows, he's a wealthy man (here an apprehensive glance towards Jeremy) … but I've got to make it good to him somehow. That's why I've come to you … To get it off my chest … and … can you think how I can do it? Give it back?'

'Which is more important to you – you paying back the money or your partner receiving it?' asked Jeremy.

'I hadn't thought. It's like I want to punish myself … fine myself. But he needs some satisfaction, too.'

'Satisfaction?' murmured Jeremy.

'I don't know. I owe him something, not just money. But I still can't tell him.'

'Fine yourself?' Jeremy hinted.

'Ten thousand … twenty thousand these days … and I'd double that. I want to hurt myself. I'd double the amount.'

Jeremy smiled. 'Zacchaeus …' he began, but went no further. It was not the time to explain an obscure biblical reference.

Ten minutes later, Alan left. He shook the Vicar's hand warmly. 'I think you've done it,' he said. 'A thousand thanks.'

So it was that some time later Jeremy found himself writing a letter to a man he'd never met:

"I enclose a receipt for $40,000," he wrote, "in your name". The anonymous donor wished to support this charity and was pleased to do it in your name for reasons I cannot divulge. I'm afraid I cannot give you any more information …".

A Taste of Mammon

By no means did Father Jeremy think of himself as without reproach. After all, he had spent many years in the outside workforce before he was ordained, and in that time engaged in many pursuits that people in the pews don't ordinarily connect with the clergy.

One of these was that he would stake a small wager on the horses every now and then, and this tendency to chance his fortune didn't altogether leave him when he turned his collar round the other way.

Not with the racetrack, however. The fact is that he occasionally bought a ticket in the Saturday night's Tattslotto draw. This would happen only when he was out of town. Jeremy dare not be seen coming out of the Tattslotto agency down the road from the church. Parishioners might excuse him, but critical non-church-goers never!

It so fell that one Saturday night Jeremy won a fourth division prize. 'Well I never!' he exclaimed to Josie. 'A hundred and forty dollars!'

'*Some* of your money back,' retorted Josie, who was not enamoured of Jeremy's weakness in this regard.

Jeremy ignored the barb. 'What can I do with it?' he asked, in genuine uncertainty. 'A windfall like this. It's not easy.'

'We need a new toaster,' replied Josie. 'I could name a dozen things in the kitchen alone.'

But Jeremy wasn't listening. He chuckled to himself. 'Windfall! That's just the right word.'

Josie looked puzzled.

'Windfalls. Fruit, you see,' Jeremy went on. 'The first fruits are to be given away. It's in Leviticus.'

Josie thought for a moment. She too knew her Bible. 'But that was given *to* the priests, not *by* them!"

Jeremy laughed again. 'You sound very rabbinical. No, we'll give ten percent to the church, for a start. Make it an extra twenty dollars in the plate tomorrow.'

'You've still got a hundred and twenty on your conscience,' said Josie. 'Take off the money you spent on the ticket – another twenty dollars, was it? - and there's still a hundred dollars.'

'I don't like to spend it on myself,' Jeremy went on. 'Or ourselves,' he corrected himself.

Josie gave in. She knew her husband too well to argue. 'You'd give away the shirt from your own back,' she muttered, and picked up a fresh ball of wool. 'I'll leave you to sort out your own moral problem.'

But Jeremy wasn't listening. 'Shirt, you said?' he asked dreamily, and soon drifted off to his study to attend to some of the odds and ends of the next day's services.

'Well?' Josie enquired when they met for their pre-bed cocoa. 'Decided how to disburse your riches?'

'Yes!' Jeremy replied with unwonted firmness. 'I have! Shirts! I'm going to buy two new clerical shirts. Heaven knows I need them … and they're not for myself, really, are they!'

'No, dear,' said Josie. 'Not really for you.'

'By the way, Jeremy added, 'listen carefully to the epistle tomorrow.'

Josie looked up.

'2 Corinthians 9. It's about God loving a cheerful giver.'

A Troubled Mind

Father Jeremy was on his way to see Charles. Charles Fraser, having reached eighty, had given up his various roles in the parish, but remained Jeremy's most trusted confidant.

Jeremy's difficulty was that he had been reading a book that had caused him much anxiety – 'Joshua', by Joseph Girzone.

'You see,' Jeremy explained, once the two were comfortably seated and the tea poured, 'he says the Church has drifted right away from how it was in the beginning. All the churches. We need to get back to how it was in the early church. The churches have put a kind of straitjacket on the people and stifled their freedom. All rules and regulations.'

'And why are you so upset?' asked Charles.

'Because he's right. Absolutely right. Listen to this.' Jeremy pulled out the book and turned to a part he had marked. *"Jesus preached a message of freedom. Religious leaders have twisted his message into a code that is irrelevant to man's nature and thereby restricts the natural freedom people should enjoy. This is what makes religion seem like a burden to people."* He's right,' Jeremy continued. 'We've got it all wrong.'

'And what about yourself?' Charles asked.

'I'm part of it all,' Jeremy replied with some force. 'I'm part of the problem. I'm one of the hierarchy, like a …' - he struggled for the word – 'like an overmaster.'

'A very benevolent overmaster, then,' Charles replied. 'Here, let me take a look,' he went on.

Charles read the passage and glanced through some of the following pages. At length he looked up.

'There have to be some structures, you know,' he said. 'Even the disciples appointed a committee to run the food supply. And I should think you're glad you've got an archdeacon to help with the organizational things while you get on with the rest of your job.'

Jeremy looked up. 'What *is* my job, then,' he asked, urgently.

Charles was silent for some time. 'Jeremy,' he began, 'when I look at the parish, I don't see people cowed by rules and regulations. I see happy people loving and caring for one another. Here, see these words on this other page. You must have missed them. *"In a real community of Christians, the people are the heart of the community. They are allowed to live freely and plan their own lives as Christians, and to build up their own lives as God's people."* 'The Sabbath was made for man, not man for the Sabbath,' Charles added.

'What's my role in that, then?' Jeremy asked.

'Why, it's there in the next sentence. *"The pastor is for them a gentle guide, offering advice and counsel and direction when needed."* That's just what you do, Jeremy. You give us all the freedom to be ourselves. You let us each discover the riches of the Spirit. And our own path towards God,' he went on.

Jeremy was in sombre mood at home that evening. And Josie noticed him slipping a slim volume high up onto the back shelf.

Church Parade

Ronnie Sanders was the Youth Group leader. An excellent young man in all respects … except that Father Jeremy would have liked to see him come to church occasionally. His church, that is. Ronnie attended a vaguely evangelical church some distance away 'Baptist, Church of Christ, something like that,' Jeremy muttered to Josie.

Still, Jeremy was happy with the way things were. Ronnie never missed a Friday night meeting with the young folk in the Parish Hall. Mrs Streatham, a retired primary school teacher was always there, too, in order to fulfil all righteousness. And Ronnie took the children skating and to youth rallies and to properly-screened picture shows … and the annual Sunday morning church parade at St Michael's.

Today was the day. Fifteen youngsters, looking very much at home in their strange surroundings chattered and swapped places interminably in the front seats while a handful of their parents sat at the back looking uncomfortable. The regular congregation cheerfully accepted being moved out of their regular seats. Ronnie and Mrs Streatham sat beaming amongst their protégés.

"Stand up.' Ronnie's hoarse whisper echoed through the church as Jeremy entered to begin the service. The Youth Group banner was presented, the children and the parents welcomed, and the first hymn announced: *A Man there lived in Galilee*. All the hymns this morning came from the 'Hymns especially suitable for Children' section of the hymn book. The adults sang lustily.

For today the lectionary was abandoned. The Bible readings were brief and deemed appropriate for the occasion – the call of Gideon from Judges, chapter 6, and the account of the boy Jesus in the Temple from Luke, chapter 2. Both offered opportunities for an appropriate sermon.

For his address, Jeremy abandoned the lectern for once and stood in front of the altar rails. He told the full story of Gideon, 'the mighty man of valour', and reached a telling peroration in which he exhorted the people, young and old, to venture into the full possibilities of life in the confidence that God would be with them as he was with Gideon.

After the final hymn, Ronnie unexpectedly launched into an impromptu talk to the children, in which he urged them to give their lives to Jesus, which Jeremy took as rather a back-hander to himself. However, the children listened intently, and Jeremy noticed that one or two of the parents looked distinctly moved by Ronnie's remarks.

Afterwards there was a special morning tea. The regular attenders did their best to engage the newcomers, while children ran around with cakes and fizzy drinks. It was a long time before everyone had left.

'Well done, Jeremy,' said Tom as he was leaving. 'A great service. You certainly have a way with children.'

'A way with children?' Jeremy was shocked. It was the last of his accomplishments in his own eyes.

Josie had overheard the remark. At home, she prodded. 'You certainly have a way with children,' she repeated.

They both burst into laughter.

Last Rites

Jeremy was in a deep dream, the sort of dream that Jacob dreamt in the wilderness. Into this dream, however, came the insistent jangle of the telephone. It took a moment to distinguish reality from the insubstantial pageant of the dream … then, the bedclothes thrown off, Jeremy staggered unsteadily into the hall, and stabbed at the phone. 'Father Jeremy speaking.'

'It's Mark, Father. I'm at the hospital. Roger's son. Roger Jennings. I'm with Dad. They don't think he'll last through the night.'

'I'll come straight away,' said Jeremy.

Jeremy glanced at the clock. Two-thirty. And Saturday night. First service at eight. 'Why didn't they tell me?' Jeremy complained to Josie, as he struggled into his clothes. 'Roger Jennings. Nobody told me he was ill.' There was no reply. Josie had slipped back into delicious sleep.

Jeremy found Mark and his two sisters by the bedside. They talked in hushed voices, as if not to intrude on the old man's privacy as he went through his last hours.

Roger himself was breathing deeply. Jeremy spoke some words of greeting and the old man's eyes opened. He appeared startled, as though awaking from a dream, as though already seeing into another world. Then he recognized Jeremy.

'What are you doing here, you old rascal?' said Jeremy, as he took his hand.

Roger grinned, and began to speak. But his words were muffled and erratic, and Jeremy, with the others, strained forward to hear.

Jeremy couldn't make out what it was. 'I think he said something about being with Doreen,' whispered one of the daughters. Doreen, their mother, had passed away some years earlier.

Roger gave up the struggle to talk and lay back, seeming to stare into the distance.

Jeremy again took his hand. 'I'm going to say some prayers for you, Roger,' he said, 'and give you God's blessing.'

By the time Jeremy had finished, Roger had sunk into what seemed like a deep sleep. Jeremy made the sign of the cross on the old man's forehead, then leant forward once more.

'*Receive him, Lord,*' he murmured, '*as a lamb of your own flock,*

as a child of your own creating

as a soul of your own redeeming

and grant that whatever sins he may have committed

through the weakness of his earthly nature may be forgiven

and that he may for ever enjoy

the clear shining light of paradise.'

Jeremy left a little later. 'He was a good man,' he said to the others. 'And you have been good to him.'

Jeremy drove home through the deserted streets of the town. It was an eerie scene. His thoughts were on the hospital bed behind him and the little group gathered there.

The call from the family came just as Jeremy was leaving for the early service.

Roger had died a little earlier.

'We will dedicate our eucharist this morning to our old friend, Roger Jennings,' he told the people.

There was a very subdued mood throughout the service.

What's in a Name?

Father Jeremy had always carried some uncertainty over the question of baptism.

He was aware that some of the other clergy thought he was dangerously liberal in the matter. He knew of cases in other parishes where baptism had been denied to children. Some families had even come to him as a result, and that had caused him much anxiety.

He knew, too, that some of his brothers and sisters of the cloth insisted on baptisms being conducted during the main service on a Sunday morning. Jeremy heartily agreed with that, but had many times agreed to have the baptism on a Sunday afternoon where there were special reasons.

It was with these things in mind that Jeremy called on the Smith family. He knew nothing of them. Susie Smith had rung and arranged for Jeremy to call late in the afternoon, after Sam had got home from work. He found Sam and Susie and their small bundle, Alexander. The baby's traditional name instantly endeared him to them.

All went merry as a marriage bell (not that there had been a marriage, but that was of small moment for Jeremy). A date was fixed. Yes, Sunday morning, in the ten o'clock service was fine. Yes, the godparents themselves were baptised. About a dozen people were expected to come.

The snag arose when Jeremy asked for the baby's full name. 'Alexander Buddha,' replied Susie.

Jeremy's pen froze in his hand.

'Buddha?' he checked. 'B-U-D-D-H-A?'

Yes, 'Buddha' was what they had named their little one. 'Alexander Buddha'.

A deep frown came over Jeremy's visage.

'Er … Is that a family name? Buddha?' He was dimly aware of a footballer who had been called 'Buddha'.

No, they just liked the name. They liked the sound of it. It went with 'Alexander'.

'Do you know what it means - Buddha?' he asked them. The baby was becoming restless in his mother's arms.

They'd heard the word before. Did it have something to do with ancient times? With India perhaps?

Jeremy explained about Buddha. 'You see why I'm hesitant,' he said. 'Baptism is a Christian sacrament. We are admitting Alexander into the family of Christ's church. I don't think we can use a name that is so non-Christian.'

But Susie were adamant. She had set her mind on 'Alexander Buddha'. There was an impasse.

Jeremy was not used to such a situation. He was a mediator at heart. Hadn't Josie once called him 'the Great Compromiser'? These were lovely people. Alexandra was a lovely baby.

There was a moment of deep silence. Then Jeremy, the Great Compromiser, had an idea. They would allow the full name on the baptism certificate - indeed he was already registered as such - but in the service itself he would use just his first name, 'Alexander', and he would be actually baptized in that name alone.

Sam and Susie gave in. Jeremy left with smiles all round.

It was a lovely baptism, but as he walked home afterwards, Jeremy wondered what some of his colleagues would have thought of the morning's proceedings.

The Vicar's Afternoon Tea

The tentacles of the parish reached into some strange places. One of these was the sewing group that met in Rene Woodward's home on the second Wednesday afternoon of each month, at two o'clock.

The connection began long before Father Jeremy had ever come to the parish. In those distant times, a group of women from the church had met in one another's homes to make baby's clothes to pass on to the hospital and the Infant Welfare Centre for needy families.

It had become known as the Church Ladies Sewing Group, but over the years the church component had been diluted to such an extent that the only one with any sort of contact with the church was Mary Nestle, and even she was a rare attender.

Nevertheless, the title was proudly borne by the women involved – the Church Ladies Sewing Group. One of the things they insisted on was that the Vicar should be invited to join them for afternoon tea at the end of their session. Not every month, but three times a year, in March, July, and the Christmas break-up in December.

Jeremy, who had a strong sense of duty, never failed to appear. But there was a problem. The afternoon tea was always laid out beautifully – always six plates of goodies: jelly cake, shortbread, yo-yos, sponge, melting moments, and something savoury. How much trouble these women had been to, he thought, and especially for him, it seemed.

Jeremy also had a strong sense of not offending anyone, so he was careful always to take one item from each plate. He knew how prickly some people could be if what they had brought along should seem to be rejected.

Jeremy felt very ill-at-ease about this. 'They must think I'm a terrible glutton,' he would say to Josie on his return home, and indeed Mary Nestle one Sunday after church did make a snide remark about his sweet tooth.

It so chanced that on one of these occasions, as Jeremy was accepting the last of his six duty-offerings, that a remark from one of the women led him to believe that it was not actually the case that six different women had brought the six dishes. Rene Woodward had made them all!

The information burst on Jeremy like a thunder-clap. 'What a fool I've been,' he thought. 'Here I've been bursting myself for appearances' sake while all these women have been taking me for a second Henry the Eighth.'

What to do? He decided to bring it into the open. Were the plates all made by Rene? Yes. Had no one else ever brought anything? No. Had they been thinking he was a more-than-hearty eater? Yes. Laughs all round at this point.

Jeremy told them how he'd been eating so much so as not to offend anyone. There was great jocularity.

Next Sunday, at morning tea, there were many remarks about Jeremy's appetite. 'Here, Vicar,' people kept saying. 'Have another biscuit.'

The word had got around. 'Those women!' Jeremy muttered, and shook his head.

The Things that Matter Most

Father Jeremy never thought of himself as a counsellor. True, he had done a CPE course – Clinical Pastoral Education – as part of his training, so that he had some idea of how a counsellor should operate. But he used mostly his common sense in dealing with difficult situations – 'and his feeling for others', Josie would have added.

Now, Jeremy was faced with a difficult situation, not from his parish, but from his own family.

Jeremy had a nephew, Justin – his sister's son – who was an aspiring Olympic athlete. He had won State sprint titles and was on the verge of selection in the national team. His whole life centred on his athletic career.

But into this brilliant expectation came tragedy. A debilitating illness put him out of all consideration and meant that he would never compete at top level again. His life had collapsed in ruins.

'Please go and talk with Justin,' his sister pleaded. 'He's always listened to you.'

Jeremy had always felt a huge reluctance to act as 'the priest' in his own family, especially in a case like this where so much expectation was placed upon him.

Nevertheless he went straight round to the hospital, giving no thought to what he could say to comfort his nephew. 'The Spirit needs some room to move,' he said to Josie.

Justin spoke intermittently and morosely about what had occurred.

'Justin,' Jeremy said, after a long period of silence. 'Can you think back ten years or so to when you were eleven or twelve years old?'

Justin looked at him.

'What did you think then – about your future, about your life?'

Justin had a ready answer. 'Why, I was mad on science. I was going to discover a cure for cancer – to begin with!'

Jeremy noticed a smile on Justin's face as he lay back on his pillows.

After a time, Jeremy asked, 'And what if we look ahead ten years? What do you see for yourself then? You'd be in your thirties. Fifty or sixty years of life ahead of you.'

Justin took a long time to reply. 'I've never thought that far ahead. I've never thought past winning gold at the Olympics.'

More silence.

Then, dreamily, as if he was speaking more to himself, Jeremy went on, 'I read somewhere once that the one true satisfaction you can have is to come to the end of your life and be able to say to yourself that you have done some good in the world …'

Justin seemed to take this in. 'It reminds me of a song I once heard,' he said. 'Aled Jones sang it. "If I have helped somebody as I've lived my life, then my living will not be in vain". Something like that.' And he lay back again on his pillows.

Soon Justin slipped into sleep and Jeremy left.

Some days later Jeremy's sister rang to thank him for visiting Justin.

'How's he doing?' asked Jeremy.

'Things are looking up. He's talking about going to Uni to do Science.'

One Day a Week Job

The twenty-fifth anniversary of Father Jeremy's ordination was approaching. His mind went back to that pivotal event in his life, and particularly the words of his ordaining Bishop: 'Say goodbye to working for yourself and bid welcome to a life of working for others.'

'He didn't say how much, though,' he said. It was Friday, and Jeremy was sitting at the lunch table with Josie. 'How *much* work!'

Jeremy had his diary open in front of him.

'Look at this, he said:

Today. 2.00 p.m. Funeral (Fred Rasmussen)

    4.00 p.m. Confirmation Class

    6.00 p.m. Wedding rehearsal (Tracey and Don)

    8.00 p.m. Wedding rehearsal (Andrew and Janine)

Tomorrow. 9.00 a.m. Wedding interview (Sharon and Dean)

    10.15 a.m. Server training (Nicole and Steven)

    3.30 p.m. Wedding (Tracey and Don)

5.00 p.m. Wedding (Andrew and Janine) (attend Reception)

Sunday. 8.00 a.m. Holy Communion service

10.00 a.m. Holy Communion, with baptism (Simon Patrick O'Dea)

11.15 a.m. Interment of ashes (Virginia Lomas)

12.00 noon. Baptism (Amber Larsen)

1.30 p.m. G.F.S. Executive, Parish Hall

3.00 p.m. Home Communion (Geoff and Wendy)'

Jeremy read the details while Josie looked over his shoulder. 'And there's not much let-up next week,' he said.

'But you're not complaining, are you!' Josie said.

'A clergyman never complains,' said Jeremy with a wry smile.

'And you've got a day off on Monday,' Josie added.

The phone rang. Josie answered, then handed the handset to Jeremy. 'It's Fred, about the Ordination anniversary.' Fred Naismith and Jeremy had been ordained together and remained fast friends.

Josie stayed to hear what was being arranged.

'How're things? What are you up to?' she heard Fred say.

'Nothing much,' Jeremy replied. 'How about you?'

On the Tuesday following, Jeremy went to the local Rotary meeting. He wasn't a member, but it was a Friends Night, and Jack, Jeremy's churchwarden, had asked Jeremy to come as his guest.

Jeremy knew quite a few people there, and enjoyed the formality of the evening set against the obvious good fellowship amongst the members and their guests for the night.

After the meal and welcoming speeches, guests and members mingled informally around the room. Jeremy, as the local Vicar, was the centre of a good deal of attention and banter.

'Glad you could come, Vicar,' said one man unknown to Jeremy, in a slightly mocking tone. 'I thought you might be too busy on a Tuesday night.'

Jeremy smiled politely.

'The Mothers Meeting's tomorrow night, then?' the man went on.

Jeremy stiffened, but said nothing.

The group began to break up, but as he turned to move away, the same man said something Jeremy half-heard, about how good it must be to have a job with one day on and six days off. Some of the others laughed with him.

Jack was in high spirits in the car on the way home. 'Good night?' he enquired.

'Very pleasant,' Jeremy replied. 'Thanks for asking me.'

'It's good for church and state to get to know each other,' Jack said with a smile.

Jeremy smiled, too, but for a different reason.

The Very Special Dinner

Geoff and Wendy were parish treasures. Now in their late 'eighties, they no longer joined in parish activities, but were remembered lovingly for their past services. They continued to support the parish financially from their considerable resources. Jeremy visited with the sacrament every second Sunday afternoon. Recently, Jeremy thought he detected signs of Geoff becoming a little forgetful.

After one of these visits, as they were having the regulation cup of tea, Jeremy remarked that Josie was shortly to have a birthday – a 'big birthday', ending in a zero. They were to have a weekend in town by way of celebration.

Geoff instantly replied that he wanted Jeremy to take Josie out to dinner at the Menzies Room in the Hotel Plaza, at his expense. He and Wendy had dined there on their fiftieth wedding anniversary. Jeremy was to spare nothing, but have the finest meal, together with the best wine, and he, Geoff, would repay their bill on their return home.

It happened just so. Jeremy felt very uncomfortable about it, but Josie insisted that they treat themselves as never before in their lives … and, after all, it was her birthday! It was a meal to remember for all time. Entrees, mains, dessert, and different wines to accompany each course, served in the most opulent manner. Jeremy was rather lost in the ordering, but Josie knew just what to do.

The meal over, Jeremy fumbled for his credit card. 'Add ten per cent to the bill,' Josie said. 'We can't be cheapskates.' Jeremy was aghast at the total figure, but Josie assured him that Geoff would expect nothing less.

It was a wonderful weekend, but after their return, as the day for his Sunday afternoon visit to Geoff and Wendy approached, Jeremy felt more and more uncomfortable. Nevertheless, he knew he had to take Geoff at his word and report fully on the meal and the cost.

The day came. The Communion service was completed. The three of them sat around with their tea and cake, Jeremy in a conniption as he waited for Geoff to ask about the dinner.

No word was said. Eventually, Jeremy raised the matter. If I don't today, it will be harder next time, he thought.

'We had our dinner at the Menzies Room,' he began, cautiously.

'At the Plaza Hotel?' Geoff answered. 'I know it well,' he went on. Actually, Wendy and I dined there for our Golden Wedding anniversary last year.'

Silence ensued. Jeremy began to fear the worst.

'Yes, you mentioned that last time I was here,' he prompted.

Geoff's face remained unmoved.

'I thought you would be pleased that we had dinner there,' he said, weakly, as a last attempt.

That was the end of it. The conversation moved on to other things.

'You know how Geoff's memory has been a bit fuzzy lately,' Jeremy said to Josie, on his return.

There was no need to say more.

Josie stared at her husband as the penny dropped. She took his hands in hers and they burst out laughing.

Father Jeremy on Thin Ice

Father Jeremy was not a scholar. He knew it, and so did his congregation. However, they enjoyed his homely sermons, which left them room to think and draw their own conclusions.

It was the long green season after Pentecost, and, with few major festivals occurring, Jeremy felt his sermons were rather in a rut. As he sat down to prepare his next Sunday's sermon, his eye fell on the fact that the day, 31st August, was St Aidan's Day. An idea stirred in Jeremy's mind. He would put aside the usual Sunday lectionary and preach a sermon on the early English saints, with specific reference to St Aidan. 'It will be good for people to realise how much we owe to our ancestors in the faith,' he said to Josie.

The trouble for Jeremy was that he knew next to nothing about St Aidan, but with the help of Cross's 'Dictionary of the Christian Church' and other dusty tomes he pulled together a sermon of sorts. 'Please God, let no-one ask any questions,' he muttered.

Just before the ten o'clock service, two visitors introduced themselves – John and Ingrid Saunders, from England.

'Visiting our daughter in Semmens Street,' they said by way of explanation. Both were very distinguished in appearance, and John in particular spoke with an impeccable Oxford accent.

As the service went on, Jeremy's mind became fixed on the visitors. 'My sermon! My sermon!' was echoing through his head. Once a thought slips into one's mind, it can grow and grow until it becomes a fixation. By the time Jeremy began his sermon, he was sure that his visitor, John, was an Oxford University Professor.

As he stumbled his way along, Jeremy's confidence in himself sank more and more. John by now was not just a university Professor, he was Professor of Early British History. He hardly looked up from his notes. He dared not look in the newcomers' direction. The sermon finished in a series of monotone clichés straight from the text books. How awful it seemed to Jeremy!

The rest of the service was no better. Jeremy's mind was now set on the moment when he would greet the visitors as they left the church. What would they say? Would John think him an ignorant colonial ninny? Would he be critical or patronizing, perhaps?

The service somehow over, the people filed out towards the narthex for morning tea. The Vicar seemed abstracted this morning, they noted, but nothing was said. From the corner of his eye, Jeremy was aware of the two English visitors coming nearer and nearer. Then the moment came. There was a beam in John's eye that Jeremy was unable to interpret. He held out his hand. Jeremy weakly responded.

'There's one great benefit to being here in Australia,' John said, cryptically.

Jeremy couldn't fathom what was to follow.

'Benefit?' he croaked.

'Yes,' came the follow-up. 'We get to see "Neighbours" twice a day.'

Jeremy felt a vast weight lift from his shoulders.

'Um. Twice a day?' he said. 'Indeed. How good! Do come and join us for morning tea.'

Jeremy Wept

'Do you know Elsie Maddocks?' It was after the ten o'clock service and Margot Stainsbury leaned towards Jeremy at the church door.

A blank look came over Jeremy's face. 'Should I?" he replied.

'In McLean Avenue. It's just that she was sounding off in the street about you the other day.'

'About me? Who is she?'

'I'd better not say any more,' Margot went on. 'I've said enough,' and hurried away.

Jeremy spent an anxious afternoon. He found an 'E Maddocks' at 16 McLean Avenue in the phone book, and on Monday morning he drove to see her.

The house was typical for the street – post-World War Two, double-fronted, brick veneer, rather down at heel. He felt unwelcome as he walked to the front door and rang the bell. Mrs Maddocks was some time coming.

The door half-opened. A sharp-faced elderly woman looked suspiciously at him.

Jeremy put on a bright front. 'Mrs Maddocks?' he began. 'I'm Father Jeremy from St Michael's.'

'I know who you are, don't worry,' replied the woman.

Jeremy was momentarily taken aback. 'You're a member of our church?' he said at length.

'You could say that,' came the reply.' My family have been at your church for longer than you would know about.'

Jeremy remained silent, confused.

'My father was an altar boy at your church before you were born,' Mrs Maddocks went on.

Jeremy felt the animosity almost physically. How could he get over her antagonism?

"I'm very sorry I haven't been to see you,' he ventured. 'I really didn't know of your connection with the church.'

'But you know of theirs well enough,' came the riposte, and the woman gestured towards the street.

Jeremy looked blank.

'Don't think I haven't seen your car at Number 21 often enough. At those people's. You don't have any trouble visiting them.'

Jeremy looked behind him. Number 21? The Collings, of course. He should have realised.

'I see you coming and going there, all smiles and how-do-you-do. Never a thought for me.'

Jeremy stood just where he was for some time. How could people be so unkind, so ungenerous, as this woman? He thought of her wrapped in her prejudices, feeding on her sense of injustice. How contrary to everything he had spent his ministry trying to instill in his people.

'I'm sorry you see things that way,' he said at last. 'Is there any way I can make up for my oversight?' Oversight. He chose the word carefully.

He knew it was a hopeless case, and the woman's response showed that to be so.

'I've had done with you all,' she declared. 'I've seen enough of the hypocrisy of the church.'

Hypocrisy? Jeremy could hardly cope with what he was hearing. A verse sprang into his mind: "The tongue is a restless evil, full of deadly poison".

He stepped back. 'I'm sorry, Mrs Maddocks,' he said. 'Perhaps we should leave it at that.'

'Yes, I think you should,' she replied.

And as he turned to go, she turned the knife. 'And I wouldn't ever bother calling again.'

Jeremy sat in his car and wept.

King for a Day

A big day was looming.

It was the fifth Sunday, so the two morning services were combined … AND the Bishop was coming to preach and to dedicate the new window in memory of two former parishioners.

Jeremy stirred uneasily as he woke that morning, and, sure enough, the telephone rang. Seven o'clock.

It was the Bishop's wife. The Bishop had woken with his voice absolutely gone. It happened sometimes. He couldn't come this morning, but Jeremy should just go ahead with the dedication himself.

'The dedication,' said Josie, who had joined him. 'You have to do it; there's family coming from South Australia.'

'And I've arranged for the local paper to be there,' added Jeremy.

Then a worse thought struck him. 'The sermon!' he bellowed. 'What can I do for a sermon?'

In an emergency, there's nothing a man needs more than a resourceful wife. Josie was up to it. 'You go to your room and get the dedication ready,' she said. 'I'll write a sermon.

At nine o'clock we'll have breakfast, and Bob's your uncle.'

The church was crowded. Despite not having the Bishop, the congregation was in high spirits. The singing was splendid. The readings were beautifully read. The Sunday School children behaved well as they filed out of church for their activities in the Hall. Jeremy preached with rare aplomb. He made several acute points about art works helping to raise our hearts towards God, yet the real church, he said, lay in the people rather than in the building. And he finished with a fine tribute to the couple who had provided the window and in whose name it was to be dedicated.

The dedication itself was brief but sincere. Jeremy made a pleasantry about himself acting for the Bishop. The final hymn, 'Worship the Lord in the beauty of holiness,' brought the service to a fitting conclusion.

The mood was continued at Morning Tea. The Ladies Guild put on a special spread. The visitors were immensely pleased with how everything had been done. 'A wonderful morning', they said. 'We're so pleased we came all this way.'

Jack, the Vicar's Warden, made a bee-line for Jeremy and Josie. 'Wonderful service, Jeremy,' he said. 'Everybody's saying so. And a great sermon. How do you do it?'

Jeremy looked bashful and made sure he didn't catch Josie's eye.

Molly, the Sunday School superintendent, came up just then. The people hushed; they seemed to know something was afoot.

'The children were very busy this morning, Jeremy' she said. 'They've made something for you. We think you made an excellent Bishop,' and she took from the large bag she was carrying a Bishop's mitre made from hard cardboard and held together with sticky tape. She placed it on his head.

The crowd dissolved into laughter.

The aftermath came the following Wednesday morning. 'Look at this!' shrieked Jeremy to Josie. He held the local paper in his hand. Splashed on the front page was a photo of Jeremy wearing his mitre.

'*OUR OWN BISHOP*,' the caption read.

Father Jeremy Finds a New Role

The congregation of St Michael's was decidedly Anglo-Saxon. Father Jeremy felt vaguely disappointed about this. If we live in a multi-cultural country, we should have a multi-cultural congregation, it seemed to him. There were many reasons to have a sense of pessimism in the church, and here was another of them. Still, what could he do?

There were smatterings of other cultures from time to time. Take Amara for example. Amara and Ross and their family had been quite regular ten o'clock attenders for several years. Amara had been raised in an Indian family in Fiji, had come to Australia to work, and then married Ross, inheriting his two children. They were then blessed with a son of their own. Ross was a slow and gentle man, and left most of the family decisions to his wife.

Latterly, things had been going wrong in the household. Two of the children had been ill during the winter. Their precious cat had been run over and killed. Amara herself had fallen on the back steps and dislocated her arm. A small fire in the kitchen stove had done some damage … and soon after that heavy rain had caused a flood in the front room.

One Sunday morning, Ross asked if Jeremy could call in during the week.

Jeremy listened to their tale of woe, wondering all the while what he could do to help. The matter was decided for him. 'Amara, you see,' said Ross with some diffidence, 'Amara would like you to come and exorcise the house.'

Jeremy was visibly taken aback. Never had such a request been made to him. Confused thoughts tumbled into his mind. Did this come from some lingering Hindu element in Amara's upbringing? Was exorcism allowed in the Church? Would he have to ask the Bishop? Where could he find an exorcism liturgy? But he could see that Amara was determined that this should be done, and, in line with his innate disposition to help someone in need as the first reason for action, he heard himself agreeing. Besides, he was being asked not to exorcise a demon from a person, but to drive out evil spirits from a house. He would come the following Sunday afternoon, he said, and carry out the exorcism.

Dressed in choir robes and purple stole, Jeremy sprinkled holy water in each room as the five family members followed him. He went through the form of service he had drawn up – the Lord's Prayer, quotations from scripture, and prayers for healing of body, mind, and spirit. 'In the name of the Father and of the Son and of the Holy Spirit,' he concluded, 'I command all evil to depart from this place. May peace and wholeness here for ever abide.'

The following Sunday, Amara's eyes glistened as she thanked Jeremy with unusual emotion.

'Perhaps it was all inside Amara,' Josie remarked. 'That's all that was needed. Like faith-healing in the Philippines.'

Jeremy stood wondering. 'God moves in mysterious ways his wonders to perform,' he said quietly.

The Great St Michael's Love-In

'That's nice,' said Father Jeremy, as he put the phone down. 'Patricia and Stuart Richards want to renew their wedding vows. Remember them? The first wedding I ever took. At All Saints. It's their silver anniversary.'

'I'll never forget,' said Josie. 'St Valentine's Day it was, actually. You didn't check the bridegroom's shoes. The best man had written *HELP* on the soles.'

Jeremy shook his head. 'I'm older and wiser now,' he returned.

'Maybe we should join them,' said Josie. 'Renew our own wedding vows.'

Jeremy stroked his chin. An idea was forming.

'Jack,' Jeremy began. He had cornered the Parish Council chairman after the morning service. 'What do you think about this? There's to be a renewal of wedding vows the Sunday afternoon after St Valentine's Day. Two couples. What if we put it out for everybody? Everyone in the parish.'

Jack took some time to put this together. 'You mean open slather. Any couple who wanted to?'

Jack was wondering what his wife, Doreen, would think. 'We wouldn't want to hurt anyone. Like widows and spinsters – and Trevor.' Trevor was the parish's elderly confirmed bachelor. 'They might feel left out. Drive home the difference, you know what I mean.'

'I've thought of that,' replied Jeremy. 'We could have another ceremony to begin with. Celebrating all relationships past and present. Honouring them before God.'

'LGBQTI as well?' Jack queried.

Jeremy thought for a moment. 'Anyone who wants to hold their relationship before God and ask for his blessing. That would be my idea.'

'All right. We'd be breaking new ground, but we'll put it to Parish Council,' said Jack.

It was the breaking of new ground that worried Jeremy just a little. However, he talked it over with the Bishop, who couldn't find a problem. Then, Parish Council agreed. And Josie, too. All hurdles were cleared.

Somehow the plan got into the local paper. 'Sounds like a Korean love-fest' said one letter to the editor, but others wrote in support.

The phone calls and emails began to arrive. 'They're all sorts,' Jeremy said in dismay. 'Catholics, Unitings, Lutherans, Any Other Religions, None-That-I-Can-Think-Ofs.'

'You started it,' said Josie, rather inconsiderately. 'You can't say no now.'

'I'll send them all a copy of the service beforehand,' said Jeremy, 'and tell them that if they can't agree with honouring their relationship before God and seeking his blessing, they shouldn't come.'

The Great Day arrived. The church was packed. Jeremy, with Trevor assisting, led the preliminary liturgy. Jeremy spoke about God calling people into relationship, using Genesis 2:18 as a text – 'Then the Lord God said, "It is not right that the man should be alone. I will make him a helper as his partner"'.

Then followed the Blessing of Wedding Vows, led by Patricia and Stuart, with the whole church full of couples calling out their responses. Josie slipped from her front seat and stood beside Jeremy.

'I think we did the right thing,' said Jeremy afterwards. 'I think it worked.'

'How romantic you are!' replied Josie.

Jeremy was left wondering just what she meant.

With All the Hopes of Future Years

"*May we speak the truth in love*", the opening prayer had said.

Still, Father Jeremy was deeply anxious. The moment had come when the Parish Council would decide whether he or she would be granted an extension to his appointment as Vicar of the parish.

The Diocesan regulations provided that a Vicar should not remain in one parish longer than ten years, except that he could have a three-year extension with the approval of both Parish and Diocese.

Ingrid was one of the younger members of Parish Council, and very progressive in her views. 'Much as we love our Vicar,' she was saying, 'the rule about moving on after ten years is a wise one. Clergy get stale after a time, surely. It's good for them and it's good for the parish to have a change, to recharge batteries, and allow new thinking to be brought in.'

Jeremy was studying the meeting papers with fixed intensity, not daring to look up or to show his feelings. Still, he thought he noticed some heads nodding while Ingrid was speaking. His thoughts began to drift, actually. He found himself back at his Induction into the parish. He remembered the thrill of taking up his work amongst these new friends. He reflected how his enthusiasm had settled into a steady rhythm of mutual co-operation and caring, how he had come to know so many families as if they were his own, how comfortable he felt amongst these people now deliberating on his future.

His musings were interrupted by the voice of Jack, the Vicar's Warden, the Chairman of the meeting. 'I don't disagree with what you are saying, Ingrid. I can't help thinking, though, of what we would lose if Jeremy were to go. Have any of you known anywhere else the warmth we have here in our parish? Do you know any other group of people so contented as we are? How much we have come to depend on each other? And where does it come from? Where does it begin? We don't have far to look.'

There was silence for a time. Old Cedric added a word. He spoke more to himself than to the others: '"Therefore encourage one another and build each other up,"' he said. '1 Thessalonians 5:11.'

No one else offered to speak.

'We'll take a little time to think,' Jack said. All sat in silence. A wordless prayer was on Jeremy's lips.

The motion was put. There were no votes to the contrary. 'Jeremy will remain as Vicar of St Michael's,' said Jack. There was a warm round of applause. Jeremy looked around the room, shaking his head in acknowledgment.

There were more congratulations as the meeting broke up. Ingrid was foremost in her warmth.

Jeremy walked across the yard to the Vicarage. Josie had supper ready, and the kettle was on the boil.

They looked at each other. Josie immediately understood.

'Here,' she said. 'Cinnamon cake and cocoa.'

'What could be better!' replied Jeremy.